# Our Special Treasure

By Katie Robertson

Katie\Robertson

ISBN-13: 978-0615801667

ISBN-10: 0615801668

Questions or comments, contact: katiejr@comcast.net

For I know the plans I have for you declares
the Lord, plans to prosper you and not to harm
you, plans to give you a hope and a future.
Then you will call upon me and come and pray
to me, and I will listen to you.  You will
seek me and find me when you seek me with
<u>all</u> your heart.

Jeremiah 29:11-13

Psalm 33:11

The Plans of the Lord stand firm forever,
the purposes of His heart through all
generations.

# Long ago God had a special plan to make you.

Psalm 19:1

The heavens declare the glory of God;
the skies proclaim the work of His hands.

The same hands that made the sparkling stars,
the trees, and mighty mountains,

made YOU!

Psalm 139:13-14

For you created my inmost being,
you knit me together in my mother's
womb.  I praise you because I am
fearfully and wonderfully made;
your works are wonderful I know that
full well.

God made you in a <u>very</u> special way:
pretty green eyes,
a cute nose,
hair that curls,

and a smile that brings <u>so</u> much joy!

Psalm 23:6

Surely goodness and love ❤ will follow
me all the days of my life, and I will
dwell in the house of the Lord forever.

God wanted to put you in just the right home.
A home that was safe, cozy, and warm,

and where you could learn about God.

Psalm 100:

Know that the Lord is God.  It is He who made us, and we are His; we are His people, the sheep of His pasture, Enter His gates with thanksgiving and His courts with praise; give thanks to Him and praise His name.  For the Lord is good and His love endures forever; His faithfulness continues through all generations.

We are _so_ thankful that God chose us
to be your mommy and daddy.

We love ♥ you _so_ much and want to take the best
care of you.

Ephesians 6:1-2

Children, obey your parents in the Lord, for it is right. Honor your father and mother — which is the first commandment with a promise — that it may go well with you and that you may enjoy long life on the earth.

The first time we saw you
we knew that you were very
♥ SPECIAL! ♥

Zephaniah 3:17

The Lord your God is with you. He is
mighty to save. He will take great
delight in you, he will quiet you with His
love. ♥ He will rejoice over you with
singing.

Philippians 4:13

I can do everything through Him who gives me strength.

You're bigger now - you can walk, run, jump, play, talk, eat, sing and even ski! ♥

Colossians 2:6-7

So then, just as you received Christ Jesus as Lord, continue to live in him, rooted and built up in him, strengthened in the faith as you were taught, and overflowing with thankfulness.

But as you grow we love you even more!

Mark 12:30-31

Love the Lord your God with all your heart and with all your soul and with all your mind and with all your strength. The second is this: Love your neighbor as yourself. There is no commandment greater than these.

Just know that we are always here for you... ♥

...to love you, hug you, and to help you to be <u>all</u> God wants you to be.

John 3:16

For God so loved the world that he gave his one and only Son, that whoever believes in him shall not perish but have eternal life.

We want to teach you all about
God - His awesome love ♥, how He
protects us and keeps us safe,

and how He will <u>always</u> be with you.

Believe in Jesus... and you will be saved!
Beloved, Let us love ♥ one another... Jesus is our strength in trouble...
The disciples were filled with joy!
Jesus is our strength
Live in peace with one another!

1 John 4:7-8

Dear friends, let us love one another, for love comes from God.  Everyone who loves has been born of God and knows God.  Whoever does not love does not know God, because God is love.

There is no one else like you!
You are truly our special treasure
and always will be! ♥

# Meet the real little girl this book is about..

Little Karina

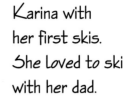

Karina with
her first skis.
She loved to ski
with her dad.

Below left:
Karina and her mom
share a book.

Below right:
Karina and her dad
on a boat ride.

# When she got bigger...

Karina had fun helping her mom in the kitchen.

Karina and her sister had a party with their American Girl dolls.

Karina liked to "cook" and make things on the beach.

# From the Author...

Katie Robertson and her family live in Gig Harbor, Washington. Katie has a degree in Elementary Education from the University of Washington. She enjoys being a mother, running, boating, drawing, and volunteering for Young Life (a non-denominational Christian organization).

*"I illustrated and wrote this book for my daughter Karina - our special treasure - when she was two years old. I really wanted her to know about God's amazing love and the plan He had for her. We enjoyed reading this book together when she was little and as she grew. We also enjoyed reading Bible stories and Bible verses. I would write a Bible verse on white paper and let her color and decorate it and post it for us to see and talk about. We would also work on memorizing them together. This was the beginning of anchoring her in faith. It is truly an amazing gift and privilege to help ground our children in faith and share with them how special they are!*

# Ideas for anchoring your children in faith

1. It's never too early to start talking to kids about the Lord, helping them to know how loved they are, and what a special plan God has for their lives. (Jeremiah 29: 11-13)

2. It's never too early to start helping kids memorize scripture. From age two and up kids easily repeat short phrases and songs. This scripture once hid in their hearts, will stay with them their whole lives. (Psalm 119: 11)

3. Teach your kids the simplicity of prayer: that they can come to the Lord with all of their cares and concerns, and also with gratefulness for the many blessings of life. (I Peter 5:7)

4. Teach kids to combat fear with what is true…you can nip anxiety in the bud by teaching kids to hold firmly to truth rather than the imagined "monster under the bed." (Philippians 4: 8-9)

5. Teach them the importance of time with the Lord. Kids love the idea of finding their own special, secret place where they can meet for quiet time with Him. Give your kids a children's Bible and a journal and teach them to write their thoughts and prayers in it. Help them to cultivate a personal relationship with God. As they get older this can be a habit that keeps them anchored. (Matthew 6:6)

6. Focus on the faithfulness of God in your own life and share stories about answered prayers, "God moments", and stories from the Bible or things you read about others, of His faithfulness. (Lamentations 3:23)

7. Make the most of every opportunity to show kids how God is in the details of life, and impress upon them how deeply He desires to be in relationship with us. Don't be shy about helping kids invite Christ into their heart. (Deuteronomy 6:6-9)

8. Take time for daily devotional readings together, talking about the Lord openly and showing how He is real. (Proverbs 22:6)

9. Point out the wonders of creation and the amazing patterns and things in nature that point to designs of a Master builder and Creator. (Psalm 19:1-2

10. Make learning about God fun with songs, plays, puppet shows, and movies. (Colossians 3:23)
11. Be intentional about giving kids a wide exposure to faith activities through involvement like church, summer camps, special speakers, and concerts. (Hebrews 10:23-24)
12. Treat your family like a team: get your kids to support each other like they would team mates. Eat together. Make time for shared activities, vacations, play and conversation. (Ephesians 4:2-3)

In memory of
Karina Jean Robertson,
our special treasure